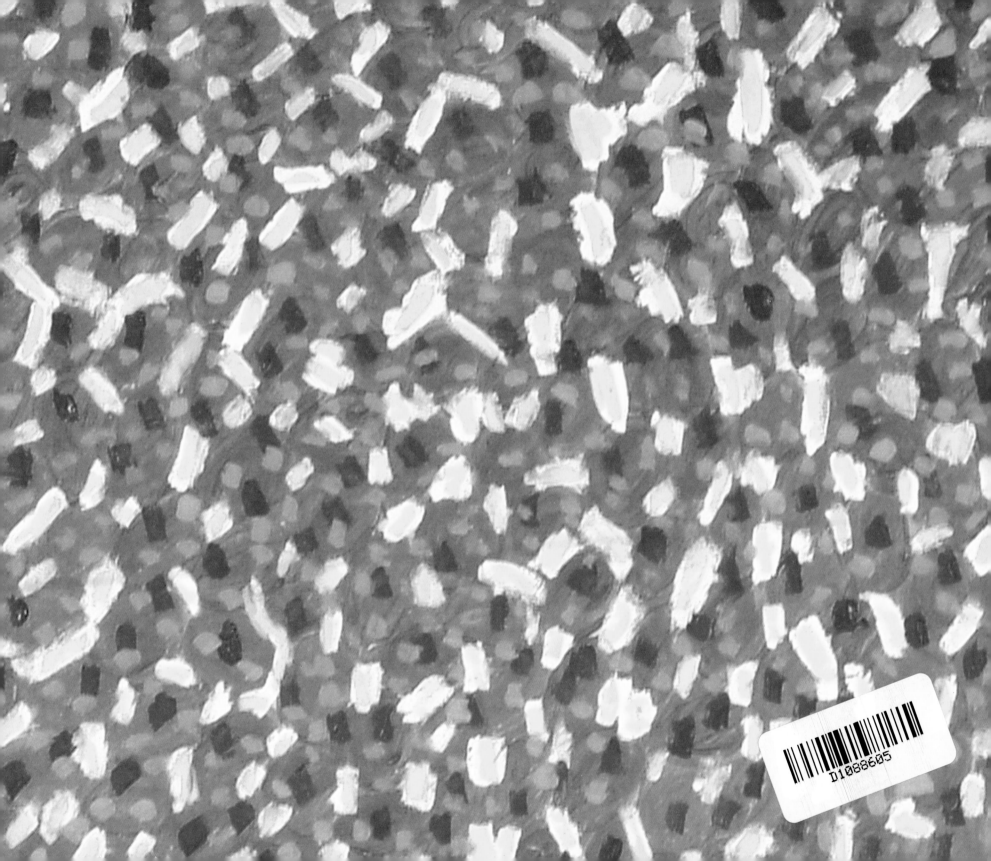

_____

This Book is Mine, Mine, Mine!

Just Be Yourself !

Written by Steve Tiller   Accompanied by the art of Harry Teague

MichaelsMind

Steve Tiller, Author
Harry Teague, Artist
Robert Cremeans, Creative Director / Art Director
Kathryn L. Tecosky, Editor
Victoria DeLoach, Photographer

Special thanks to: Our Families, CCAD, David & Melissa Abbey, Alana Shepherd, Mike and Shannon Francklin,
Barbara and Barry Klein, Terri Potter, Ben Tiller PC tech wiz, Blue, Noah, Hayden, Brooke, Rachel, Katie, Alan
Carter, Mary Zeman, Brian Bias our Apple guru, Scott Stettler at Brand EXX.

Library of Congress Cataloging-in-Publication Data
Tiller, Steve

Summary:
A book that allows us to celebrate the differences that make each of us unique and special.

ISBN 1-932317-10-4
[1. Individuality - Children's Fiction.   2. Self Esteem - Fiction.   3. Interfaith -Diversity

Printed by
Regal Printing Hong Kong

Harry Teague's Paintings were created with acrylic paint on mat board

Visit us for fun and games at:
www.michaelsmind.com

Or visit Harry and Diannia at:
www.harryteague.com

To our family and friends with a special thanks to Charlene Ediger who helped take Harry's boredom into a new direction with lots of color!

-Harry and Diannia Teague

To the Great Architect of the Universe, and to the family and friends that He has built into the life of Steve and Lizabeth.

-ST

Just be Yourself
Hold your flag high!
Shout to the Heavens
Aim for the sky!

Just one on the planet
Exactly like you-
There won't be another
Can never be two!

Show off your colors
Always be proud!
Don't let yourself
Get lost in the crowd!

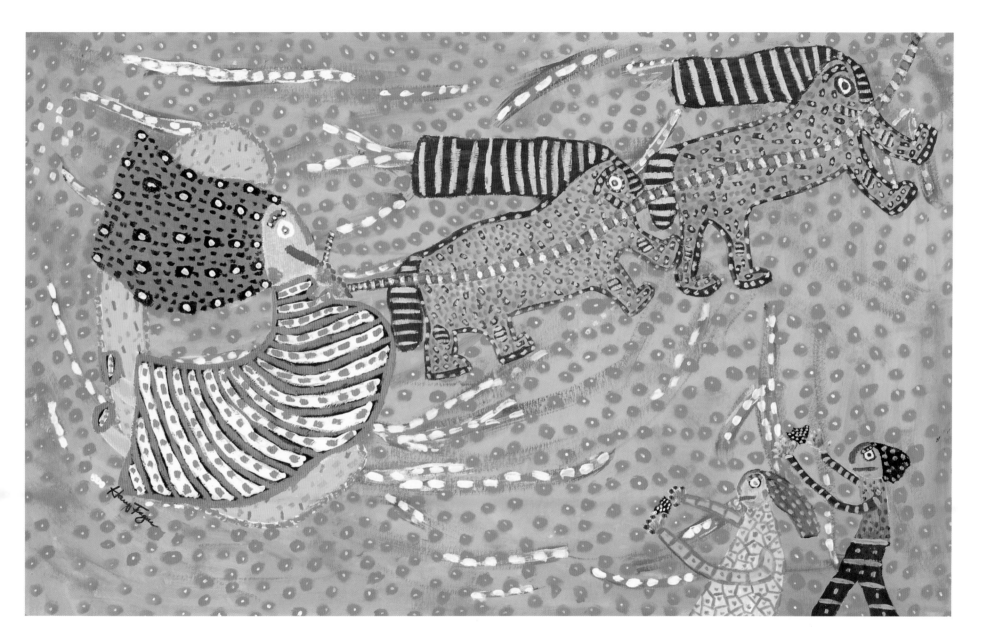

Away She Goes 2004

We all want to know
Can you run fast?
Do you play football?
Think you can pass?

Beat your own drum,
Toot your own horn!
Discover the reason
Why you were born!

Can you play catch?
Think you can hit?
Can you play first base?
Did you bring a mitt?

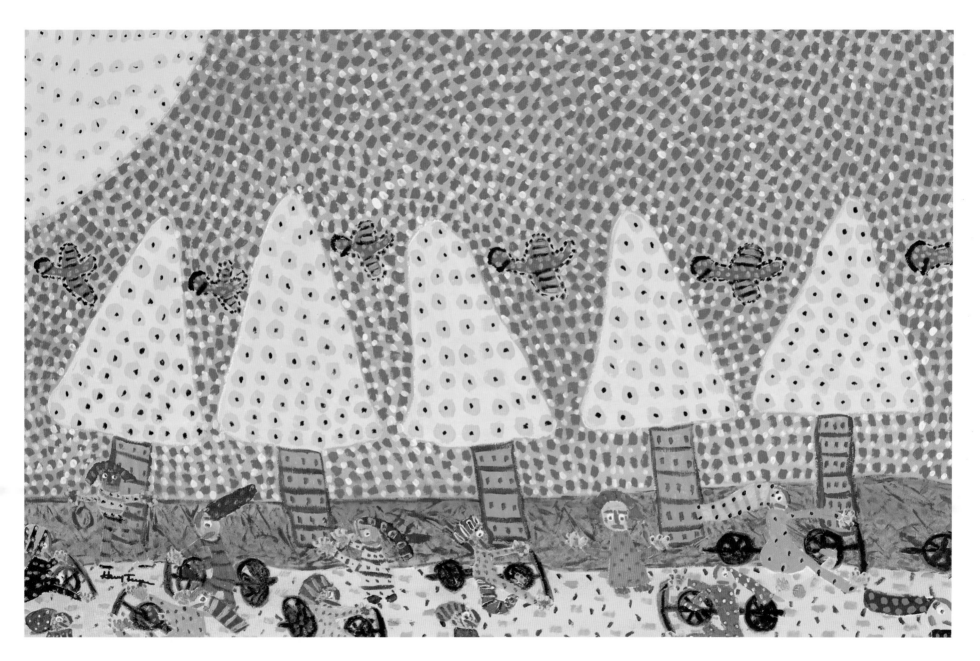

Fun on the Wheels 2004

Feel you don't know
Who you might be?
Just keep living life
Then, you will see!

Things get easier
With practice you know.
You'll learn to do it
Just give it a go!

Hold on real tight
Keep your eye on the wave.
Trust in yourself
Be bold and be brave!

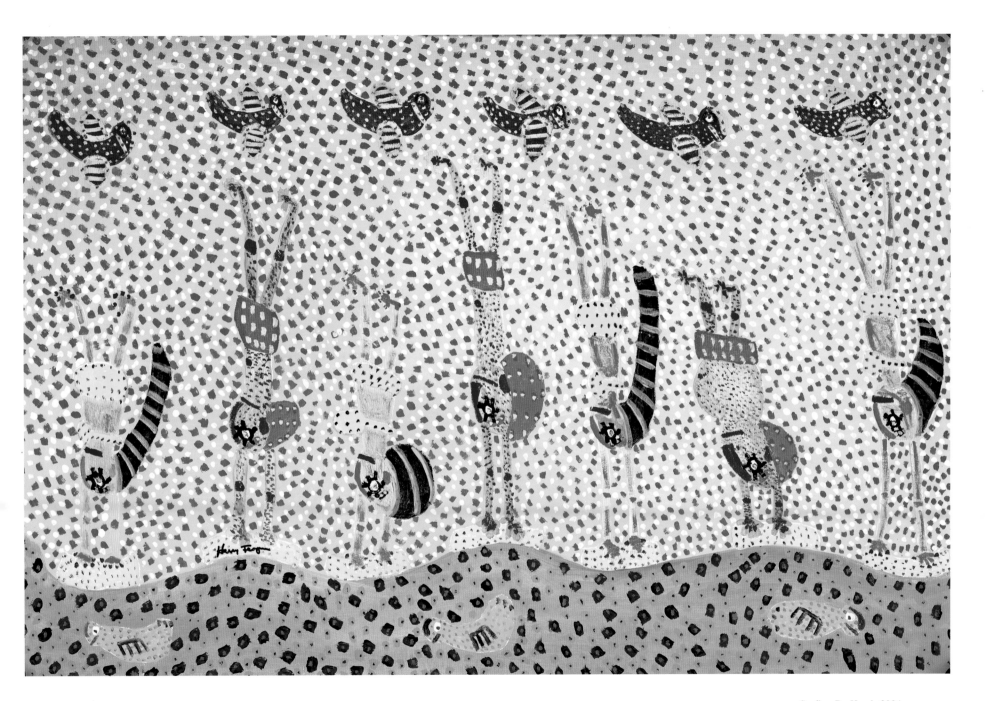

Surfing By Hands 2004

Look on your inside,
What's hidden there?
Got any feelings,
You'd like to share?

Think you're a lion?
Let loose with a growl!
Have a wolf in your spirit?
Get out and go howl!

The Pilot of Life
Wants you to fly high!
Take wing together
To soar through the sky!

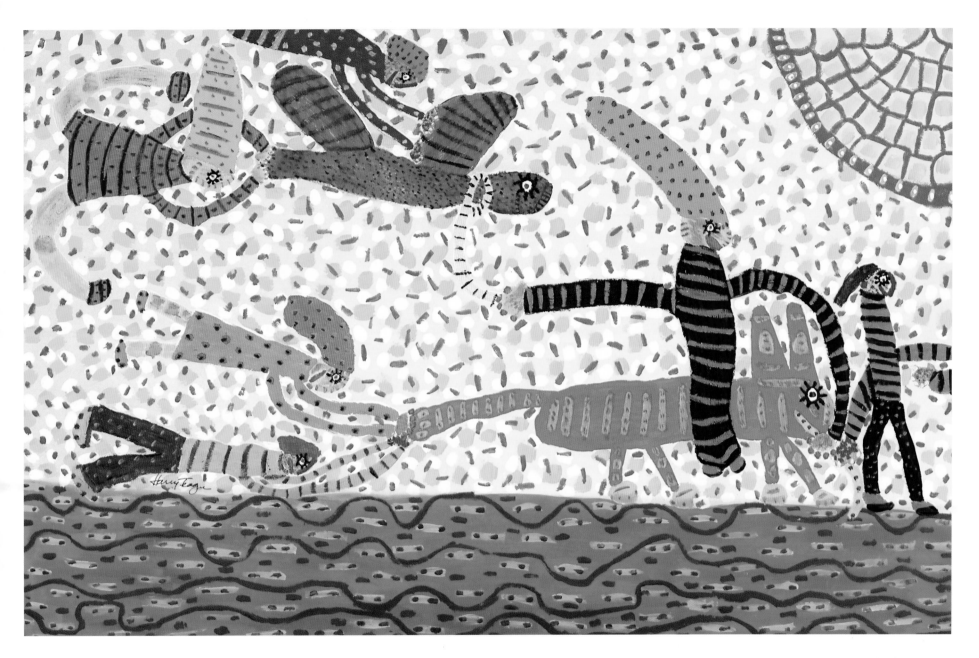

Taging On

Express what you feel
You've big thoughts to share,
Don't hide them inside
We really do care!

If you have a light
Hold it up tall,
Let it burn brightly
To shine on us all!

Let the great things inside
Sparkle through you,
We all want to see
What you can do!

Guess Who 2004

If you are a princess
And dress up's your thing,
Grab a gown, get a wand
And, go find some wings!

Always be nice
Don't feel remorse.
But, set your own sail,
Sail your own course!

We're not all the same
We like different things!
So, fly your own kite,
Tie your own string!

I See It 2004

Put chocolate on bacon
Try blueberries on ham,
Make pancakes in purple
Bake cakes in a can!

Think you're an artist?
Do you like to paint?
Don't worry about lines!
Does the smell make you faint?

Let your balloon fly
When the winds blow,
There is really no telling
How far it might go!

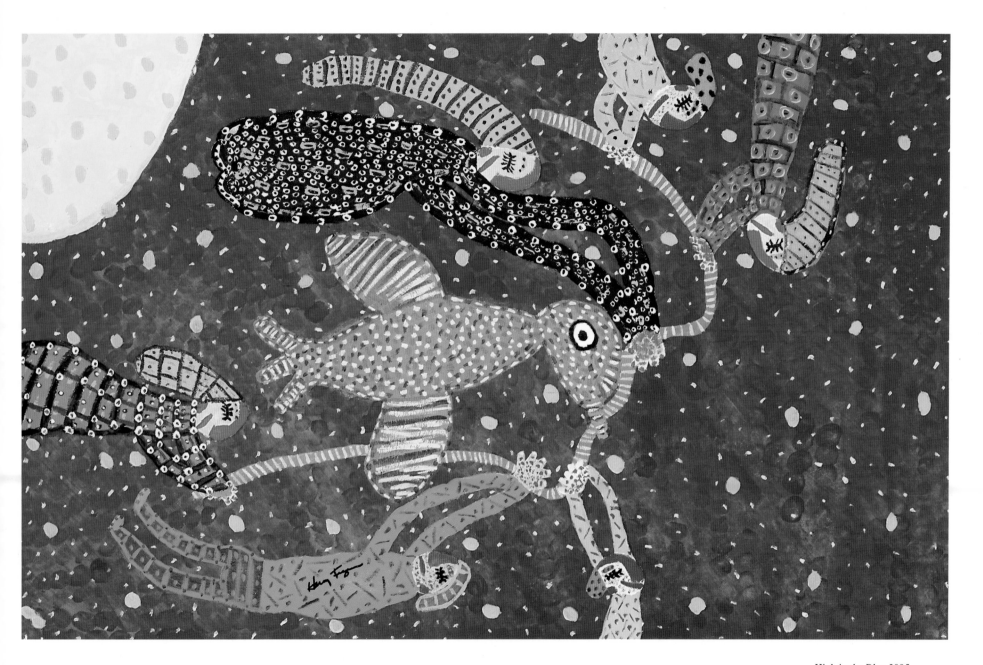

High in the Blue 2005

Can you play tennis?
Do you like to chew gum?
Don't you love food?
Do you ever feel dumb?

I'll tell you a secret
I've felt that way too.
Until I remember
The great things I can do!

All of us are terrific
At some stuff we do!
And, all of us stink
At a lot of stuff too!

Fancy Flight Plane 2004

All of us have talents,
Each one is unique!
You're great at something
That's what you seek!

You might be an astronaut
And visit the stars,
Or work in a factory
Making really cool cars.

You could be a soldier
To help keep us free,
Or maybe a diplomat
Who has the Queen in for tea!

Green Airplane 2004

Do you like playing
Tag in the yard,
Screaming like crazy
Running real hard?

Would you rather find
Some quiet nook,
Curling up quietly
To read a good book?

Do you like slides?
Don't you love swings?
I like my hair
Floating like wings!

All Clapping 2004

What will you be
When you grow up some?
And how will you use
What you can become?

Share how you feel
Including those doubts,
We already like you
We'll hear you out!

Don't try to be perfect
We don't care about that,
Just be honest and caring
That's where it's at!

In My Dreams 2004

Believe in yourself,
Always be fair!
Thank others for helping,
Remember those prayers!

Need to say something?
Then, say it out loud!
You'll hear us all saying,
"You sure make us proud!"

Whatever you do
Give it your best try!
Life has no limits
So, always aim high!

Ladies Day Out 2004

Keep your confidence high
You'll be amazed!
Your skills and talents
Deserve lots of praise.

Some of us like reading
Others can spell.
Some of us have stories,
We make up and tell!

Think you can fish?
Let's bait up a hook!
Do you know about gardens?
Perhaps you can cook!

Labor of Love 2004

What is your dream?
Where's your guiding star?
You really must tell us
Just who you are!

Are you a dreamer
Of the biggest of things,
Like gigantic bridges
Or great monster swings?

Do you want to help others
Or sing on the stage?
Size is no matter
And, neither is age!

Spindle People 2004

We hear you saying
"I'm here, don't you see?
I'll make a difference
If you just follow me!"

Try to do right,
Remember to have fun!
The race isn't about winning
It's about learning to run.

Lend others a hand!
Dreams will come true
By, you helping me
And me helping you!

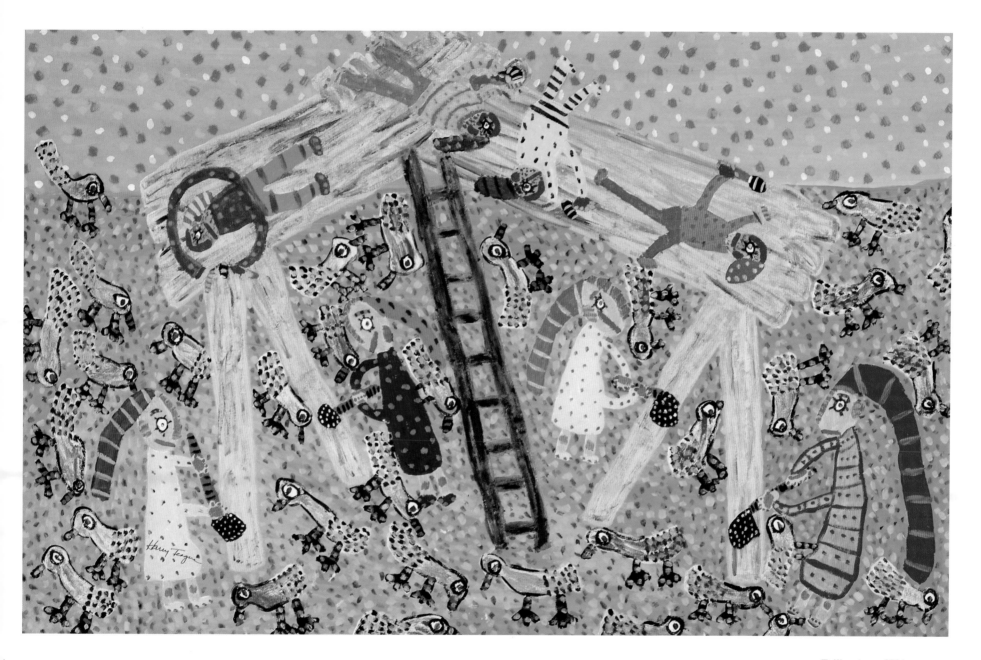

Toiling Away 2004

Who you are - <u>IS</u> your gift!
Get yourself in the light,
You are a treasure.
Unique to this life!

So, don't let us down!
The world wants to see-
How we can help you,
To be all you can be!

Just be yourself!
Hold your head high!
We know you can do it!
Now, shoot for the sky!

Cool Dude 2004

The End

Harry and Diannia Teague's world changed forever in 1990 when Harry survived a stroke. Harry's art therapy tapped into a new creative ability for expression and communication. Their efforts in art together have brought them new adventures and friends. To know them is to marvel at the adaptability of the human spirit. Each painting we see, and each meeting with these partners in art and life, is a reminder to the rest of us that when one door closes another door opens. It is with much pleasure that Harry and Diannia share with us Harry's colorful voice of art.

My wife is the love of my life. Her name is Elizabeth. She prefers Boosie which was a nickname, I call her Lizabeth because both parts of that name were some of my favorite girl names when I was growing up.

Lizabeth is a great mom. She is infinitely entertaining   She loves to talk and tell stories about what has happened that day. She will however, occasionally break out stories that she has told before. Fortunately, my memory is about as long as the hands on a digital clock, so I usually don't remember the details. Sometimes even the ones I may have heard several times before still seem new to me.

We have four, five, or six children the last time I tried to count. They move quickly. And they are very noisy. Most of the children seem to be girls. It is kind of like waking up in a forest of birds. There is the immediate and continual noise of voices at my house. It is the constant background sound of verbal negotiation for everything.

The noise begins when their lips and eyes pop open at the exact same moment in the morning, and it doesn't stop. The girls continue talking, jockeying for position, or seeking some advantage over their sisters until they are threatened with bodily harm if they do not stop talking, turn off the lights, and go to sleep at night.

I am outnumbered in the house. There is a son somewhere in this pile of stuff. But I don't see him much except in passing. And my mom is somewhere in here too. She mostly keeps busy working out or travelling. Even all the animals seem to be female.

My wife and the girls have been on vacation this week. I miss my wife. I miss the girls. It has been very quiet around here. It is funny what humans can get used to after a while. I even missed the noise.

Well, not really. I thought I did until they got back. Your imagination can sure play tricks on you sometimes.

Steve Tiller   2006

Award Winning Books by MichaelsMind

Call your favorite bookstore and give them our phone number - or you can order from us directly if you want your books autographed or personalized for gifts.

Tangle Fairies $15.95

"It's a funny little story- I am sure you've never heard. You may think it's kind of silly, probably absurd. Why- no matter if you comb your hair before you go to bed, in the morning when you wake up, you got tangles in your head!"
Reviewers said "Tangle Fairies is one of those books the kids will want to read again and again. The tiny fairies with iridescent wings and rainbow colored hair are just like children would imagine them to be."

Benjamin Franklin Award

Connected at the Heart $15.95

My daughter, Rachel, wanted a birthday story- so I put her up in Heaven waiting to be born. Rachel began to think she was going to get lost or be late until she discovers that she is connected to the heart of her mother- and she could never possibly get lost! Reviewers called it "poignant and heartwarming and suitable for personal libraries, schools and Sunday School libraries." It is a great gift for a new mom especially if there is an older child in the home, or as a gift for Mother's Day!

Writer's Digest Merit Recommendation

Henry Hump Born to Fly $15.95

Henry is a caterpillar who is suspicious of cocoons, and isn't very eager to visit one real soon! But he soon learns that if we take time to look carefully beneath the leaf – we can discover hope and optimism even in the face of overwhelming change! Reviewers said "Tiller's strength is his lighthearted approach to deep spiritual questions…Cremeans's technicolor illustrations make each bug bigger than life!"

Visionary Award

Just Be Yourself! $15.95

Let your individuality shine through in everything you do! Feel good about who you are! We are all unique with different strengths and talents. The world needs those differences expressed wisely and usefully. "There is just one on the planet exactly like you! There won't be another there can never be two! Be bold and be brave, always give your best try. Life has no limits, so keep aiming high!"

NEW for 2006

Boat & Wind $15.95

A simple conversation between a little boat and the wind about belief in things that can't be seen, Boat & Wind highlights the importance of faith and friendship in our daily lives. Reviewers said "The beautiful illustrations evoke the feeling of being at sea. Pages beam with texture and depth. The story is strong and the message important." Another reviewer said it "portrays the deep meaning of faith with childlike simplicity and unique clarity.

Georgia Author of the Year for Children's Literature

Rainbow's Landing $15.95

This book is a beautifully illustrated underwater adventure about having the courage to follow our dreams Fred the sea anemone learns the dreams we hold in our hearts can guides to finding our purpose in life. The book has a great message and vibrant, techicolor illustrations!
Reviewers said Rainbow's Landing "presents a valuable lesson with playful compassion. The illustrations keep you looking for new details hidden in the glow of the sea."

Georgia Author of Year Finalist

Santa's Red Nose Rocket $15.95

Pinky, the space alien, crash lands at the North Pole. She asks Santa about the meaning of Christmas. Santa tells the real Christmas story! "Elves dressed as kings brought him gifts from afar..." Pinky heads back to the stars spreading the message of love and hope! The best review is from people who call me for more personalized copies for the children of friends and relatives as gifts. This is a very unique and wonderful Christmas story.

Georgia Author of the Year Finalist

Inside Outside Who We Are $15.95

Diversity makes life interesting. Individual differences can also be the source of problems between people. When we look at others with our eyes -everybody is always different from ourselves. But if we close our eyes for a moment, and look with our heart instead of our mind- it turns out that everyone is really very much the same! "We are not so different as it seems. We all have hopes, we all have dreams! In your heart, you know it's true! I am very much like you!"

NEW for 2006

All of MichaelsMind books are fun. All have great illustrations. All carry a positive message. All openly discuss common values of American life such as courage, love, faith, hope, family, tolerance, and individuality. Public and Private schools use our books in value and character education programs.

Books can be ordered at our website **www.michaelsmind.com** by email **satiller@juno.com** or calling **404-314-1348** or **Fax 404-531-0360**. Payments may be made by check or credit card. Let us know if you want the books autographed or personalized as gifts. We support schools, literacy efforts and children's hospitals. Our books are often used as fundraisers.

"Thanks for your support!"